Crysse Morrison has written in various genres: her fiction has been published and broadcast and her stage plays produced, but she maintains a perverse determination to write poetry and performs at various venues in the southwest, occasionally winning local slams. A self-styled crone, she makes it her mission to give voice and visibility to the elderly, regarding dressing with inappropriate zest as a political act. Crysse intends to continue to bemuse and amuse audiences mostly much younger than herself for as long as she remembers her words.

Crumbs from a Spinning World

Crysse Morrison

Burning Eye

BurningEyeBooks
Never Knowingly
Mainstream

This edition published by Burning Eye Books 2016

www.burningeye.co.uk

@burningeyebooks

Burning Eye Books
15 West Hill, Portishead, BS20 6LG

ISBN 978-1-909136-92-2

Crumbs from a Spinning World

CONTENTS

CRONE POEMS

PROXY BOTOX

When every stupid woman in the western world
has paid for a needle to be stuck in her face
to poison her nerves so her expression is erased
of the subtle texturing of life that we call 'lines'

and that toxin has passed through the system
of each stupid woman and she's weed it all out
(and the lines are on her face again, deeper grooved
from the trauma of that unprovoked attack)

and the sewerage has been processed back into our taps,
does this mean with every sip of water,
I imbibe a molecule of Botox?
Does the unalterable logic of homeopathy decree
I too must look like a startled Cabbage Patch doll?

I have lived my life with human passion. I want my face
to show my heritage. Tears, and laughter, and all the long years
of struggle – my slow natural suicide. I don't want to erode
these tide-marks of my mortality. This is me.

BUNGEE JUMPING CRUMBLIES

Look at them! It's obscene.
Wrinklies, tottering round Topshop!
They should act their age, not their fuck-me shoe size –
should be saving their pension, not prancing at parties
wanton and plastered, still trance-dancing,
still backpacking the golden road to summer lands.

Retiring? They don't know the meaning of the word –
refusing to age gracefully, won't go quiet
into that genteel twilight good night –
collecting tattoos instead of bus passes,
puckering sundried faces for kisses,
mutton-dressed brazen lambs, perpetual Peter Pans!
What do they think they're like?

This is what I think:
I'm not a sheep to be cut and devoured.
I'm not looking for a Never-Never land.
So don't confuse me with someone who wants
to be part of those fictions – why should I
change my life-long convictions?
Curiosity. Boldness. Lust for life.

CASUAL SENIOR

I'm a casual senior, that's what I have to say
when I sign in at the gym for a workout or a swim.
It's a little bit embarrassing, announcing on arrival
I've reached that certain age of dubious survival,
and it does seem kind of strange to have to give my age
when all I'm really wanting is a chance to keep in trim.

But I wonder, as I wander, and I see that traffic warning sign,
WATCH OUT FOR THE ELDERLY – if I could act more casually
in lots of other places round this town of mine.
I could be a mooching Minnie in my crinkly's floral pinny –
shoplift vitamins from Boots – shout out in the flicks –
pull faces at the passing cars to get my third-age kicks!
And I'd snigger as the passers-by shake their heads and sigh,
'Another casual bloody senior, up to her old tricks!'

PETS AS THERAPY

*There are currently over 4,500 active PAT visiting dogs at
work in the UK, giving more than 130,000 people pleasure
and a chance to cuddle and talk to them. I actually don't
like dogs, but petting sounds attractive.*

They bring comfort to the sick and the fragile and the old,
put smiles on our faces when we're feeling past our peak.
They never answer back, they're always good as gold,
sitting close and looking gorgeous – it's the highlight of our week.
They gaze at us adoringly, they understand our woes.
That's why we love to stroke our therapeutic gigolos.

When I tumbled in the kitchen for the twenty-seventh time
my social worker – Daisy – sighed and shook her finger.
'You really need a care home, you're getting past your prime.
Let's get you sorted out, you know you shouldn't linger.'
I'd heard about those places and they sounded pretty ghastly,
just sad old ladies left alone to brood about the past... ly.

But Daisy shook her head. 'They're better now,' she said,
and she told me of a scheme that sounded like a dream.
It's provided every week to old ladies stuck in bed
and now instead of crying they're like cats that got the cream.
'It's a kind of petting therapy, they've found it's good to stroke –
but it isn't dogs they bring you, it's a handsome hunky bloke.'

I've never fancied dogs, I'm allergic to their hairs,
I can't stand the smell or the slobber or the yapping.
But with a lush young man I'll forget about my cares.
We flirt and we giggle and I never feel like napping.
My personal pet, he's Johnny Depp with extra flair
and nothing lifts my spirits like grooming his chest hair.

They bring comfort to the sick and the fragile and the old,
put smiles on our faces when we're feeling past our peak.
They never answer back, they're always good as gold,
sitting close and looking gorgeous – it's the highlight of our week.
They gaze at us adoringly, they understand our woes.
That's why we love to stroke our therapeutic gigolos.

LIFE IS GRIMM BUT NOT LIKE FAIRYTALES

You know it's a fairytale when the princess arouses
from a hundred years' coma as fresh as a daisy,
moist lips, taut breasts, and cherry nipples.
In real life each time you wake
your tits are more like chewing gum,
your peachiness more pruney –
I shall take no more naps.

You know it's a fairytale when the princess succumbs
to whines from a brute, and at her caress
he turns beautiful and pledges love.
In real life each time you offer your heart
he turns ugly and growls, 'This
is all your fault – you made me like this' –
I shall embrace no more beasts.

You know it's a fairytale when the phoenix arises,
the firebird returns, the ice splinter melts,
and the dancer with red shoes – *cuts off her feet*?
In my world there will be no such compliance,
no pragmatic submission,
no good conduct remission.
I shall paint my toes scarlet and dance like a harlot,
and when I'm too old to spin straw to gold
I shall start a sanctuary for dragons.

IT'S A SINGLE WOMAN THING

It's a single woman thing, it doesn't happen when you're
paired
and you're one half of a couple, and everything is shared.
I can buy things on a whim – for me, and not for him –
boots that break the bank, I don't apologise for swank!

I can fly off to Manhattan, wear satin nighties, be a slattern,
when you're single you can mingle, it's not a guilty sin.
You can even go on Soulmates and say you want a fling.
It's not a social crime, it's a single woman thing.

So no more appeasing and male-ego pleasing,
no more huffs and whining, I can suit myself when dining,
I can snack on Belgian chocs, or tiger prawns and shellfish –
it isn't being selfish, it's a single woman thing.

No more unexpected Spitfires, no co-dependent tripwires,
I can drop that constant look-out for enemy attack,
'cause more-than-one's a warzone, and I'm never going back.
It's a single woman thing, this sense of joie de vie.
No longer half a couple, I can be simply me.

FUMBLING WITH FREUD

JOURNEY REQUEST

I want to check in all my baggage, please.
Here's my infancy – birth trauma is in the side pocket,
those thin screams always go unheeded, no need
to tag them. Here's my teenage years – still in a strop!
This is my marriage, does it need a *HEAVY* label?
Too late for *FRAGILE*, you can hear when you shake it
how thoroughly it's smashed.
I've got a few other relationships
but I can manage them as carry-on.
This is the baggage I want to check in – just let me know
how much it all weighs, I'm ready to pay the excess.

PATERNAL ADVICE

'Don't blow your own trumpet,' my father said.
I was too young to understand metaphor (being two)
but quickly learned to mute that tiny fanfare,
bite my lip, top showing off, and hide behind
the polite and stifling mask of modesty.

And after half a century
of breathing quietly and trying to fit in
I realised what I should have said:
'Daddy, this trumpet was given me at birth
and if I don't blow it, who will?'

Trumpets and strumpets deserve to be heard.

MOTHER KNOWS BEST

It's a stage she's going through,
her mother says, and she should know,
she's known her all her puny little life.
A difficult stage. Pestering,
tugging at skirts, whining for attention.
Whimpering for love.

She's been at that awkward stage for years,
gawky and fidgety, not fitting in,
copying that common talk and sloppy slang
just because she goes to school with them.
No need to ask to bring them home, start badgering
to buy comics and all that silly stuff –
she knows we're not like that.

It's tiresome but it's that stage she's at,
reading American trash, hunched alone
with rubbish on the radio,
storming off in a huff, out till all hours,
dancing with darkies, racketing round
on the back of that tearaway's motorbike.

Ungrateful, ungracious, treating the house
like a hotel, leaving on all the lights, wanting to marry
that scruffy student with his guitar, throwing away
the chances we gave her – it's clearly a stage.
What does she think she knows about love?

All her world is a stage. Her life is a stage
she's going through, since infancy,
gathering for her performance
the props she needs: isolation, loneliness,
they are songs to fill the silence.

FIRST SCHOOL

At Rosendale Road Primary
the other children
were dreadfully common,
my mother said.

They seemed all right to me.

But I didn't seem all right to them,
so that made me
worse than dreadful,
if you look at it logically.

I was a logical child.

PUZZLED

'She thinks she's the bee's knees but she's not,'
they chanted in the schoolyard, leaving her
wondering why, with wings to fly,
bees need knees.
After all these years she muses still.
Not the bee's knees – so which part is she?
The sassy buzz... fuzzy gold body...
succulent mouth to guzzle stamens
drenched in nectar? She wants to be
the gauzy wings, translucent, fragile,
yet reaching dizzy heights, but thinks it more likely
she's only the bee's knees. Except that she's not.

ASPIRATION

Yesterday I applied to be a constellation.
They sent me a form. I needed a referee,
so I chose God, I thought he'd have some clout.
The questions were tedious and time-consuming.
Did I want to rise east or west? Summer or winter
visibility? Relationship to moon? (Cordial, I put.)
Relationship to Pluto? Antagonistic, of course.
Would I mind sharing a locker with Orion, a parking space
with the Plough? Would I babysit the Milky Way once in a while?
I did my best, second-guessing when to say yes.
But Heaven is dealing with a backlog of requests,
though I believe my application is still on file.

SELF-SUFFICIENCY

All she ever wanted was to find her feet
and they were right there, at the end of her legs,
all the time!

PLAGIARISM AND POETS

WENDY - COPING ALONE

I love the smell of you, honey,
though I haven't sniffed you yet,
but I know from the glow of your sensuous skin
it's a smell I won't forget.
I want to lick your chest, honey,
when it's warm and wet with sweat,
taste your salty sweet-and-sourness
till we're both completely powerless,
melt my moments all with you, honey –
it's such a shame we haven't met.

SENILITY, OR PUTTING ON (PAM) AIRS

I've been having some senior moments
as down the next decade I hurtle.
Like, I used Wash 'n' Wax instead of Lenor,
now my towels are all shiny as turtles.

I've ordered all the wrong photos
though I can't imagine how –
instead of that wonderful wedding
I've got thirty-two views of a cow.

I have to leave crosswords unfinished,
and names keep escaping: who's Prime Minister?
Are we still in Europe? Who's heir to the throne?
This is getting a little bit sinister.

I can manage the shopping quite well, mind,
I write it all down on a list.
Then, when I'm safely back home, I find
it's my jacket and bag that I've missed.

If you're wondering why I'm telling you this
don't think that I'm crazy, or squiffy.
It's only a senior moment, dear.
I'll know who you are in a jiffy.

VALENTINE SONG

*Winner of a BBC Valentine poem contest set by John
Hegley, who gave extra points for including references to
dog food, string, and potatoes.*

It happened on Valentine's Day –
a good day for finding a frog
morose on the pond eating Chum like a dog,
puckering up for a kiss on the nog,
promising me he'd turn princely and stay.

The day after Valentine's Day,
poised on a lily pad watching the ripples,
penicle ardour our favourite tipples,
him plopping kisses all over my nipples,
the strings of my heart twang away.

Now it's no longer Valentine's Day
my prince treats me like an old spud,
scraped and then mashed up, feeling like mud.
I handed my heart to a warty old dud.
Now I wish he would just hop away.

FAMOUS PEOPLE I ONCE SAW:

John Hegley's graciousness:

Last night I went to a reading by a popular poet.
I was intoxicated –
    by his deceptive wit
    his gloomy slyness
    his peculiar elusive rhythms
    and for other reasons.
    You can see where this is going.
    I'm afraid I may have HECKLED
    the famous poet.
I apologised afterwards, of course.
He said it was OK. Phew.
But then I thought,
does a poet ever tell the truth?

Germaine Greer's response to requests for reviews:

There once was a writer named Greer
whose views on her peers were severe.
Delusions of lyricism
had her snorting with cynicism.
Support for the sisters? Stick it up your career.

Wendy Cope's lyrical litigiousness:

A popular poet called Cope
on copyright law was no dope.
Her rhymes make a mint,
Wendy will never be skint –
can we see them online? She says, 'Nope.'

HOW DO I LOVE THEE & AFTER

LOVER'S LAMENT

Love barged into my life in muddy boots.
'You're not on the list, you can't come in,' I said
and Love just laughed, strode in anyway,
blundering through my pristine solitude,
stuck its feet under my table, chucked its socks
beneath my bed, left a ring round the bath
and didn't even care. I tell you, Love sucks.
Impudent as an alley cat, bold as a busker,
Love is a brazen thief. Stole from under my nose
my precious hoard of loneliness.

WINTER SUN

Actually
it's not all it's cracked up to be,
going to hot places in English wintertime.
You come home, brown as a lizard,
baked as sun-cracked soil,
ochre as adobe huts,
bronze as succulent sun-filled sands

and you have to put your woollies on
so nobody sees.
Except your lover
who grabs your sunglow body
as you strip and doesn't seem to care,
as if he were colour-blind. Though later
he does listen to the sun-filled journey,
he does trace the contours of your baking,
just the way you want.

HOW DO I LOVE THEE?

Reluctantly, misgivingly.
Quite confused and knottedly.
Baggage-laden, warily.
A little bit besottedly.
Seriously and frivolously.
Excitedly and satedly.
Hopefully, playfully.
Curiously belatedly.
Increasingly wholeheartedly.
Missing you departedly.

LOCAL HONEY

When she looked at him,
standing behind the counter in his black leather jacket,
she wanted to put her hand, quietly, on his
and feel his skin beneath her skin, pulsing,
ever so delicately, but she didn't.

When he looked at her,
in front of the counter, flushed with unaccustomed sun,
he wanted to throw all the customers out,
shut up the shop, and make love to her, there and then,
beside the jars of honey. So he did.

When he kissed her
she wanted to leave her friends, her work,
her land, her life, and simply live with him.

When she kissed him
he wanted to sabotage his reputation
and leave his wife. But he didn't.

MY TOP TIPS FOR AFTER HE'S GONE

The Dos:
Bounce back. Join a gym.
Buy solo meals and freeze your leftovers.

Find a face for the future. Use waterproof mascara.

Keep smiling. Watch sitcom repeats –
they're on all through the night.

Delete his number from your diary.
Erase his voice from your answering machine.

Change your routines. Avoid
places where couples laugh easily together.

Make some lists.

The Don'ts:
Go on long walks, hunched into solitude
like autumn stubble

Buy the flowers he chose for you,
arranging and rearranging their insouciant stems.

Play the CD he gave you,
over and over.

Argue in your head with him,
reconcile in your dreams with him.

Imagine hands, solid and warm,
dovetailing into yours – stare
at the full moon, fingering empty air,
as dusk bruises into darkness
and your hungry skin whines,
Are we nearly there yet?
And the answer is always *No*.

POSTMAN'S CALL

You woke me up to show me the dawn,
garish pink as girly lipstick,
glitzy as spangled sandals,
spilling like Slush Puppie all over the sky,
and what's best of all, you did it
from forty miles away, long after we'd parted.

FAIRYTALE ENDING

Once I kissed frogs
on a regular basis,
plopping my passion
on their damp horny faces.

Then pond life palled.
I sat on a lily,
looked at my life,
feeling shy, sad, and silly.

I missed that old 'reddit'
even if vigour's faded –
just a caress or a touch –
but my toad was jaded.

Once I kissed frogs
and sought princely grace,
now I just yearn for
any warty embrace.

CHARITY SHOP SHUFFLE

White boots sulk on the Oxfam shoe rack,
snubbing the elderly belts and bags which brag
their kinship of leather. The slippers are still grieving,
remembering, dimly, the fumbling of careworn feet
and a tartan blanket.

Cheap limey slingbacks, loose as undone bra straps,
make eyes at the nylon trews. Peep-toes, shocked,
mutter to each other about modern manners while
the tan court shoes fart, quietly, and pretend
it was the wellingtons.

Only the satin stilettos, red as touch-up lipstick,
watch the doors constantly, avidly, for rescue,
itching for the touch of skin, the feel
of flesh within them once more, the scent
of orchids and longing.

THREE FROM THE CYNICAL CARD COMPANY

(1)

They say love can move glaciers,
cause hurricanes and storming,
shift the contours of the world,
or was that global warming?

(2)

You take my breath away.
I wish you'd give it back.
I need it more than you.
I'm having an asthma attack.

(3)

You're a breath of fresh air in my life,
but as it's winter that's a draught.
If you think I want to stand and shiver
you must be bloody daft.

WHAT ARE WORDS WORTH?

ONOMATOPOEIA

I've always thought *celibate* an unattractive word.
It sounds like a fish. 'Battered celibate, please,
with a splash of salt and vinegar and a tub of mushy tease.'
Monogamy – what's that like, then? A bored game,
with no hotels. I've got a soft spot for *sleazy* –
it sounds silky and squeezy – but *promiscuous*
is a gorgeous word. Don't you agree? All made of
promises and kisses, and curious mystery.

I WANT TO WRITE WORDS

that are salient and succulent
and sassily succinct

that tell a tale as tall and gaudy
as Jack's beanstalk

that etch an image as vivid and indelible
as Edvard Munch's *Scream*

that smell like soft skin
and taste like ripe figs

that are pert and provocative as the 36 double-D
on page 3

words you could leave on their own in a big city
and they would glow in the dark

BLANK PAGE SYNDROME

If I wrote my poems on Ordnance Survey maps,
would they find their own way?
If I scribbled them on recipe books,
would they turn out saucy and simmering?
Would car manuals make them move less clunkily –
utility bills help them flow hot and cold –
would washing instructions keep their metre meticulous,
porn mags expose their soft and sensuous crevices,
prayer books elevate them? My poems are
written on blank paper. They gaze at me, bewildered,
not knowing what they are supposed to say.

ALPHABETTI SERENDIPITY

I like: Avocado and African baobab,
Bathing in Candlelight, Dancing at dusk.
I like Empathy and embers, Firelight and friendship
and foxes and frivolity and fingering and... frost.
I like Geraniums and greenery and Grimms' grisly tales,
Heat-hazy horizons and Indigo-sea islands.
I like Jazz and Kissing and Lipstick and lust
and Mandolin music, and Merlot and musk.
I like Nebulous nights of not doing what I ought –
Opals, openness, Parcels and paradox.
I like Quirky quips and Rock 'n' roll and roses.
I like Satire and Tattoos and my ten toeses,
Unicorns and velvet and Voluptuous vulgarity,
Wit and wild words and Xtremes of ecstasy
and I like You, yes, you, and the Zing! of poetry.

MAD ABOUT WORDS

I'm mad about words – I love to toss them out
like pearls for threading, cut and pin them –
cram them in a jar like Smarties, shake them, roll them
like marbles, whirl their kaleidoscope colours around,
spin them like tops. End-to-end them like dominoes,
pile them up like building blocks, flatten them like pastry
and pinch them into patties – fingerpaint with them,
fold the page into inkblots of splattered meaning.
Float them like ducks in the bath, chuck them
like Poohsticks in summer rivers.
Cry over their spilt milk. Dress them like dolls
in Sunday best, wipe their squeaky faces clean.
Whack them and wash them and push them through the mangle.
Leave them in the sun to dry. Press them like wild flowers,
loop them into daisy chains, chase them like butterflies,
swap them round like football cards.
Munch them like chocolate chip cookies. Tease them.
Push them off their trikes. Make them tremble.
Bury them in sand as the tide comes in. Bully them to tears,
stroke them in the night when nobody's there.
I'm mad about words. Join my crazy game tonight.

WRITING WITH A KNIFE

You dip your fine quill pen in ink and write a poem,
shaping eloquent phrases with elegance and flair,
then watch your careful words evaporate and fade.

So seize the pen again and dip it deeper,
this time using last year's blood. Score the page
with wounds... then watch your gory words blotch and smear.

Wait for a while, breathing silently, then put down your pen
and find a blade. Now cut your poems with a knife,
your words not mere marks on paper but scraped from your life.

LET US PRAISE WORDS!

Let us praise words that are fit for their purpose,
words like *floozy* and *scrabble* and *plop*.
Let us praise sibilants slithering like lizards
and clown-sounds like *eejit* and *Jiminy Cricket*,
shibboleths and oxymorons,
sweetheart words and swearwords,
innuendoes and prayer words, and insults like *nerd*,
and words like *isthmus* which are simply absurd.
Incomers like *Google* and *whatever!*
And let us not forget the fallen ones, interred
in tomes of etymology – words like *succuba*
and *florin* – we shall not speak their like again.
Invented, inverted, reclaimed, recalled,
let's revel in them all whatever their spelling.
What would we do without words? We've no way of telling.

BOX SET BALLADS

REVIEW OF *PRIDE AND PREJUDICE* (IN 26 WORDS)

Artless beauty
clearly does endear
foppish gentleman,
honest indignation
jeopardises killer lust,
making nobility of pride,
querying riches,
sensuous tension under
veiled waywardness.
Xplosive? Yes. Zounds

A COUCH POTATO'S LOVE SONG

Gene *Life-on-Mars* Hunt, Gene *Life-on-Mars* Hunt,
strapping, back-slapping, you snarl and you grunt,
a flask at your hip and a sneer on your lip.
Oh, how I envy the gun in your grip!

You sweat like a horse and stand like a stallion.
You and whose army? You *are* the battalion!
Knee-jerker, berserker, your people skills stink.
You've no social graces, your style's from the sink –

but Gene *Life-on-Mars* Hunt, Gene *Life-on-Mars* Hunt,
nothing you do could cause me affront.
Foul-mouthed and hard-drinking, in fact mostly pissed,
my pock-marked Adonis, I love you like this.

The sound of the siren, the scent of the station,
that stained camel coat, all cause me elation.
Gene *Life-on-Mars* Hunt, no one could be keener
for a ride in the back of your ratty Cortina. [1]

On the floor of my bedroom I picture your boxers
and you in my bed, passed out from intoxers.
Alas for my fantasy, dreams must unravel,
all for the want of a means to time-travel.

---

[1] For those who preferred the follow-up series, *Ashes to
Ashes*, use the '*Gene Genius Hunt*' version, and substitute
here:

The sound of the siren, the scent of the station,
that slack-knotted tie, all cause me elation.
Gene Genius Hunt, you're mean and you're rowdy –
what I'd give for a ride in your scarlet Audi.

For those who never fancied Gene Hunt, WHAT'S WRONG
WITH YOU?

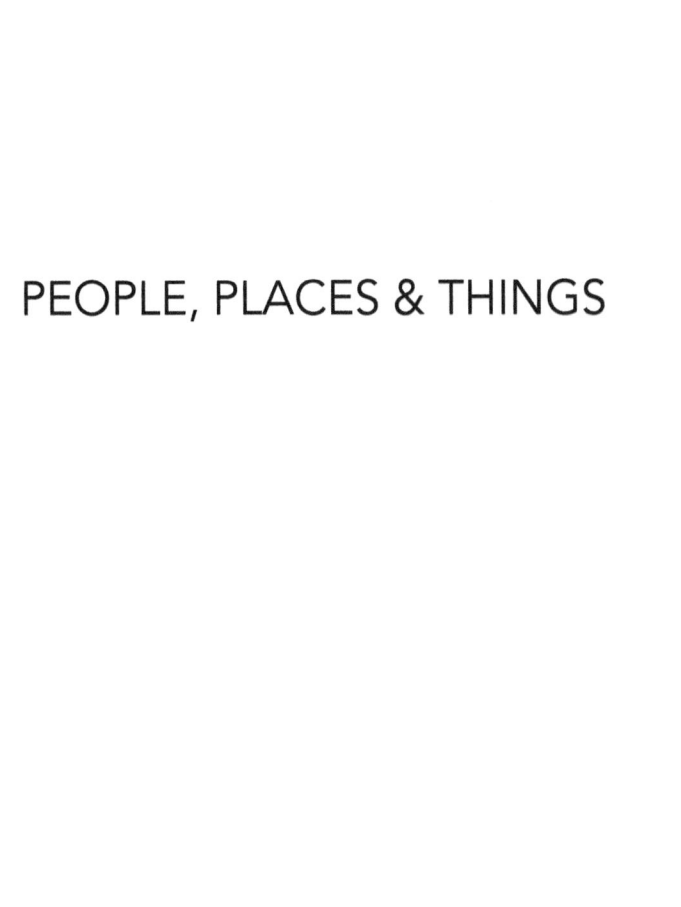

PEOPLE, PLACES & THINGS

GOD'S GIFT

smooths his hair,
slides his pale hands
down the snake hips
of his Primark suit
and smiles. That smile
would light up a disco,
illuminate corn circles,
drench the moon. That smile
once broke hearts
including his own.
God's gift rolls a fag
pursing his lips
to the song on the juke,
nostalgic for the days
when solitary women
were not all atheists...

WHY I DID IT

*Doctors examining a 36-stone woman found an asthma
inhaler under her armpit, coins beneath her breasts, and a
TV remote control in her thighs.*

– newspaper report

I am woman mountain. I swallow storms
like butterflies. Bees swarm in my eyes.
Below my arms are forests where gaudy parrots flit
through shifting shadows, between my breasts
languorous lagoons where dragons fly. My sweat
drowns oil slicks. Turtles crawl between my toes.
In my womb the tribes of lost children safely sing
while wounded soldiers blunder through the valleys of my thighs.
When I smile grim rocks sweat honey. When I shiver
the moon freezes. I munch the rolling years for fun.
I am woman mountain. I chew death like gum.

GREEK ISLANDS

They seduce you utterly, shamelessly.
Almost banal in their obvious guiles:
the moonpale beach, DayGlo blue sea,
that ceramic smoothness of the sky,
slow swirls of mist in the ouzo glass,
warm air and laughter in the night.
And everywhere, like meshing spider webs
on thorny hills, a fragility of longing.

And there is always a moment
when reality and imagination fuse.
Amber resin of then, and next...

I remember the first epiphany.
Burnished hillside, a priest
stroking a cat in the vine-leaf shade
of the monastery door.
Sun hacked the shadows.
Cicadas shrilled.
On his transistor the Beastie Boys played
you gotta fight for your right to party.

Greek islands are like that.
Virgin whores, sainted sluts.
Smells of jasmine and lust.

PLANETARY FORECAST (IN DOGGEREL, WITH GERMANE BITE)

I'm not being coy when I say, 'No presents, please,'
so don't think I'm churlish, or an irritating tease –
I love to browse the gift shop too, a real Aladdin's cavern
of bric-a-brac and gewgaws, and I nearly want to have 'em,
till I contemplate the fuel burned by the delivery truck,
which takes my mind back further, and then it runs amuck,
with thoughts of vast crates of curios criss-crossing land and seas
over thousands of miles, and I feel queasy unease
at the thought of the cultures exploited with low pay
to make ornamental knickknacks, cash-crop for Euro-play,
all so you can wrap it up, and give it to me,
and I can say, 'How nice!' and pass it on to charity…
Never mind the packaging, these gifts *do* cost the earth,
and that's why I say, 'Thank you, but I've really got *enough*!'

LOVE AT FIRST SIGHT

It was love at first sight.
As soon as the plastic ice-scraper saw my car,
it fell in love with it. It's hardly surprising – they have
so much in common: their colour (blue), their passion
for travel. On milder days my ice-scraper strokes
condensation from each window tenderly, longing for frost
when my car will want more, and soft sponge will turn to firmer grip,
decisive through stubborn windscreen resistance.
The ice-scraper, I admit, makes all the running,
but my car submits, and thaws to its yearning pressure
every time. I think they have the best relationship I know.

FIVE HAIKU

(i) Greece

Local peach, so big
I had to cut it in eight
just to quarter it

(ii) Africa

In Tendaba pool
I swim lengths. My spirit guide
is flying widths. Why?

(iii) London

Your shoes on the stair
a continuing footfall
treading absently

(iv) Devon

Irresistible
slightly wet and slightly dry
fresh-pulled raspberries

(v) Turkey

Four plump pink king prawns
lie curled, docile, basking in
serious garlic

EPILOGUE

THAT'LL DO

I want a man
who'll play Poohsticks with me
in summer rivers.
With our bodies.

WHERE DO LONGINGS GO?

Are they biodegradable?
When you chuck them from the moving car of life
do they flutter like tissues, like fruit skin, and fall
into the hedgerows, catching on cow parsley,
dripping like dew into the earth?
  My longings are red plastic.
  They will not compost down.
  I see them from miles away,
still on the verge of the road, still stubbornly blazing.

MY EVIL TWIN

My evil twin has no compassion.
Doesn't care how much she embarrasses me,
strutting forth, showing off,
letting people think she's me.
Laughing too loud in public places,
misremembering – mistaking –
missing the point
time after time
as if she doesn't damn well care.
I'd stop her, of course I would, but
she's glued my lips together,
she's smeared the mirror so I can't see myself
properly, and what's more
she's used all my own tears to do it.
    And then she's gone out dancing!
    Bitch.

FALLS ROAD, 1970

I remember going in the bakery
with one and ninepence ready in my hand,
and the assistant said, 'Bread's gone up.
It's one and ten today.' I stared.
Gone up *a penny*! That's an egg –
that's half a pound of carrots. What to do?
We must have bread. And while I scowled
and scrabbled in my purse the woman said,
'It will be two shillings soon.' And I said,
'That's ridiculous. Nobody will buy it.'

THIS IS WHAT IT MEANS TO BE A WIFE

Your finger is circled in gold, like a magic spell
in a fairytale. *Pling!* Foreverness is yours,
now you are wed. Wedlock. Locked in
to your choice. You have chosen to be responsible
no longer to yourself but to someone else.
His happiness, his comfort, his moods, his self-esteem.
You must excuse him and groom him,
anticipate, negotiate, mediate, capitulate
and wear the ring that covers your skin
and shows the world the choice you made.

And when you stop being a wife,
slide off that golden circle, break the spell,
there is still a ring, faded and frail,
on the skin that used to be yours before
you were a wife. The cellular memory stays.
You can unlock the wedlock but each day you wake
your finger still wears that phantom ring.
You'll trace the place, touching it in the night
as if it were an acupuncture point for healing.

FINGERING DELETE

Keep Behind This Line is painted on the wet black platform
and I'm waiting for the train to Howth. It's Sunday evening.
My lift has dropped me at Killester and I fumbled with euros
at the ticket counter and now stand shivering alone
in this dank November night. I watch beads of red light
on the information board flick down, the minutes descending
slow as crocodile tears, and I finger my mobile.
This is the kind of time that texting you
would melt the miles between us. I would feel
your arms around me as close as this saturating rain.

TRADE DESCRIPTIONS

I'd never buy sex.
What if it wasn't
'as described'?
How would I take it back?

FAMOUS FOR FIFTEEN KILOMETRES

'Are you that woman who walks round the town
they call the writer?' An unexpected greeting
from beyond a privet hedge. A bespectacled man
has paused in his trimming, shears aloft.
I take a breath, and a guess, and say, 'Yes.'

Like any lover, he wants to talk about writing –
his own writing and writing he's read,
and when at last I move on, I picture myself
as he'd painted me. Stomping by, jean hems
soaked with the grime of life, pockets stuffed
with coloured dreams, trailing out behind me
like a magician's bright handkerchiefs, in the wind.

TIME BEING

Time being fluid, words we etched
yesterday are ephemeral as sand.
Now is a gasp between *then*
and *next*, misremembered touching
unknowable: a slit to an abyss.

Time being momentous, now is ever.
Time, being flexible, will bend
and sway as you dance,
will soften like a fig for munching,
will glisten like gypsum in glassy rocks,
will drizzle golden in your fingers.

Time, being remorseless, will suck you dry.

JANUARY SONG

Let us praise New Year resolutions, their pusillanimous tyranny,
and let's praise their abandonment halfway through January.
Let's eat more cake, and abridge that long debate
about detoxing, how much we don't need this big glass of Pinot –
would be just as happy without it! – oh, go on then, I'm not
driving.
Let's admit this new year will be just like the last: a wrangle
with self-discipline which your more articulate decadence will win.
Let's praise the clichés and faux logic that let us off the hook:
'It is winter – be kind' – 'Men like love handles.'
Ah, the love handles of our lives, the soft slack self-indulgence
that underbellies every good intention. Let's praise *bad*
intentions.
Take courage, take heart. A toast to whatever is hidden in the
dark.

ONE LAST ONE

Time's been called but I want one more,
I'm loitering, lingering, can't go yet,
shamelessly pleading for one last poem.

Overdid it last night, guzzling words,
gorging on rhythms, feeding my addiction
till night turned to dark winter dawn.

Dozing at last, still dreaming of verse,
sticky-fingering my pen, stroking my notebook,
desperate for more, a few more words.

Still greedy and needy for another lyric fix,
just one more kick, hair of the dog that bit,
then I'm going. Promise. But first, just one

      more
        poem

.